To:

From:

THIS BOOK BELONGS TO:

_____

TRUE MEANING OF EASTER

By Melissa Wingo

True Meaning of Easter

Dedicated to my husband Gabe & my children Evelyn, Terry and Rye. I love you.

IT MUST BE SOMETHING IMPORTANT!

THEY TOOK

PALM BRANCHES

+ WENT OUT
TO MEET HIM.

JOHN 12:13A

OH NO, WHY DO THEY NOT LIKE HIM?

THEN ...

THE CHIEF PRIESTS + THE ELDERS OF THE PEOPLE GATHERED IN THE PALACE OF THE HIGH PRIEST, WHOSE NAME WAS CAIAPHAS, AND **PLOTTED TOGETHER** IN ORDER TO ARREST JESUS.

MATTHEW 26:3-4

Melissa Wingo '22

WHY IS HE
SO SAD?

MATTHEW 26:36

THEN JESUS WENT WITH THEM TO A PLACE CALLED GETHSEMANE, + HE SAID TO THE DISCIPLES "SIT HERE, WHILE I GO OVER THERE + PRAY."

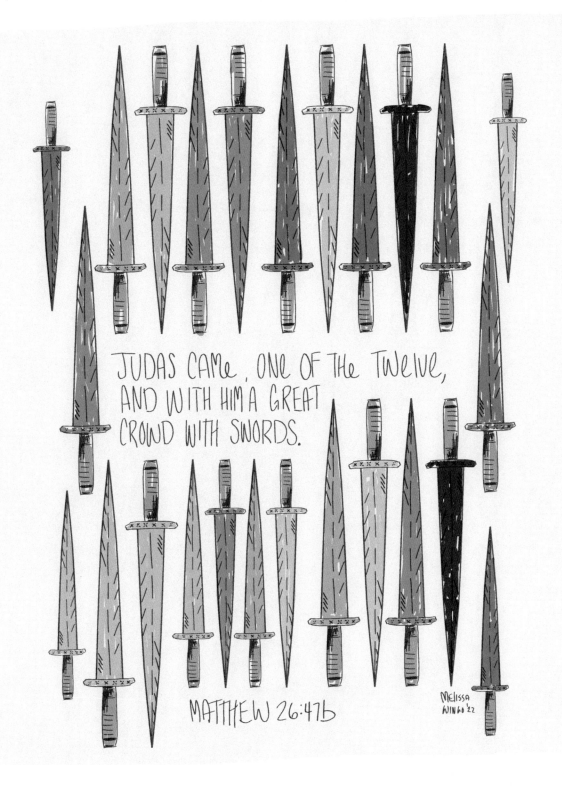

OH NO, WHAT SHALL WE DO?

When the chief priests and the officers saw him they cried out Crucify Him, Crucify Him.

John 19:6

Melissa Wingo '22

WHAT IS HAPPENING?
WHY IS THE SKY SO SAD?

I GUESS IT'S
ALL OVER.

WAIT, WHAT IS
HAPPENING?

AT EARLY DAWN THEY WENT TO THE TOMB, TAKING THE SPICES THEY HAD PREPARED, AND THEY FOUND THE STONE ROLLED AWAY FROM THE TOMB.

LUKE 24:2

EXCUSE ME, CAN YOU TELL ME
WHAT IS GOING ON?

Luke 24:6a

He is not here. He has risen!

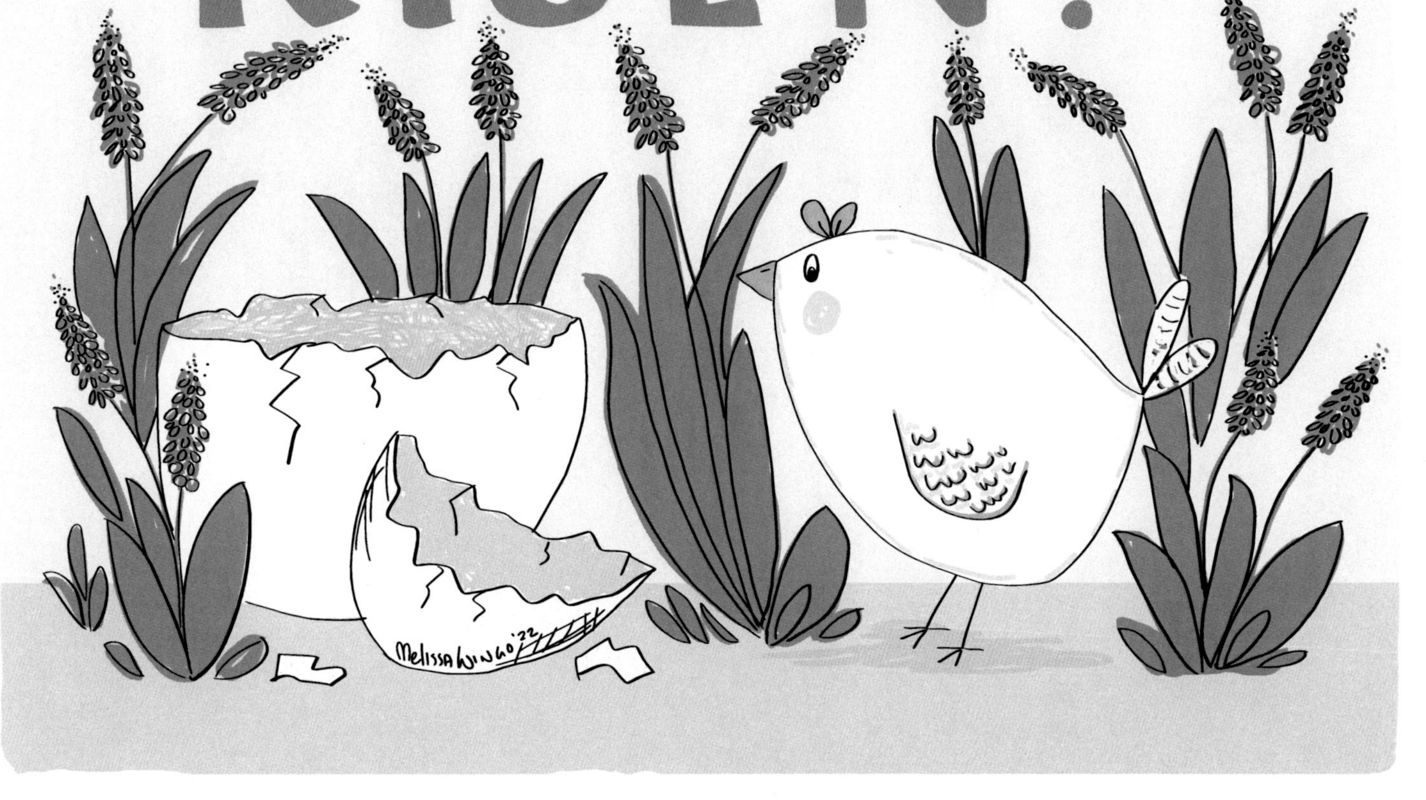

It's a Miracle!

GOD RAISED HIM FROM THE DEAD.

ACTS 13:30

I WANT TO TELL EVERYONE THE GOOD NEWS!

OH JESUS, I BELIEVE!

HAPPY EASTER!

THE END

By Melissa Wingo

My name is Melissa Wingo and I am an author/illustrator of Children's books. I live in Sunny California with my husband and three kids. I love books, drawing, the Bible, gardening and running.

Made in the USA
Monee, IL
13 March 2024

54983874R00026